THE
NEW YEAR'S EVE
SLEEPOVER
FROM THE
BLACK LAGOON®

THE
NEW YEAR'S EVE
SLEEPOVER
FROM THE
BLACK LAGOON®

by Mike Thaler
Illustrated by Jared Lee
SCHOLASTIC INC.

New York   Toronto   London   Auckland   Sydney
Mexico City   New Delhi   Hong Kong   Buenos Aires

To Matt Ringler, who makes work fun!—M.T.
To Kathy Boyer Zienty, classmate and friend.—J.L.

visit us at www.abdopublishing.com

Reinforced library bound edition published in 2014 by Spotlight, a division of the ABDO Group, PO Box 398166, Minneapolis, MN 55439. Spotlight produces high-quality reinforced library bound editions for schools and libraries. Published by agreement with Scholastic, Inc.

Printed in the United States of America, North Mankato, Minnesota.
102013
012014
 This book contains at least 10% recycled materials.

Cataloging-in-Publication Data
Thaler, Mike, 1936-
    The New Year's Eve sleepover from the Black Lagoon / by Mike Thaler ; illustrated by Jared Lee.
    p. cm. -- (Black Lagoon adventures; #14)
    Summary: Hubie has been invited to a New Year's Eve sleepover but has never spent the night away from home. What happens if he gets sick and what's all the talk about making a New Year's resolution?
1. New Year's Eve--Fiction. 2. Sleepovers--Fiction. 3. Monsters--Fiction. I. Title. II Series.
    PZ7.T3 New 2008
    [Fic]--dc23

ISBN 978-1-61479-204-8 (Reinforced Library Bound Edition)

All Spotlight books are reinforced library binding
and manufactured in the United States of America.

CONTENTS

CONFETTI

SNAKE

FROG →

CHAPTER 1
HAPPY NEW FEAR

Eric is having a New Year's Eve sleepover.

HUBIE, YOU'RE INVITED.

GUEST LIST

It will last *all* night. I've never been away from home . . . all night. Mom told me I can go, but I'm scared. Couldn't we just start with a *napover* or a *snoozeover*?

6   TOAD →

What if I have a bad dream or get sick? Mom won't be there to save me.

I will be in a strange bed, in a strange room, in a strange house. Eric says it'll be great. We can stay up till midnight and welcome in the new year. Mom says we can see the ball drop in Times Square . . . if we don't drop first. I'd like to drop out of the whole sleepover.

9

MY MOM→

CHAPTER 2
PJ'S AWAY

Mom wants me to go. She says it'll be fun. She still remembers her first sleepover. It was called a *pajama party*. She and her girlfriends played games, made popcorn, and talked all night.

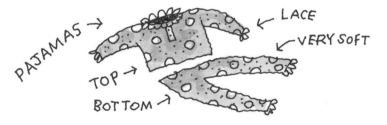
PAJAMAS →
← LACE
← VERY SOFT
TOP →
BOTTOM ↗

It sounds more like an *awakeover* to me. Besides, I need my sleep. I need my bed. I need to stay at home.

MY BED
←

11

CHAPTER 3
BLANKET SECURITY

Mom says I can take a few familiar objects for security.

THANKS, MOM.

I FEEL BETTER NOW.

Okay . . . let's see. I'll take my stuffed bear. I'll take my baseball glove. I'll take my pillow and blanket. Hey, I can even take my night-light, my bed, and my dresser.

12

FAMILIAR OBJECTS FOR SECURITY

STUFFED
BEAR

BASEBALL
GLOVE

FAVORITE
BASEBALL

PHOTO OF
MOM

PILLOW

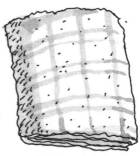

BLANKET

NIGHT-
LIGHT

BED

ALARM
CLOCK

13

I can take my computer, my TV, and all my video games.

I can take my dog and my posters. Hey, it might be easier to just stay home.

CHAPTER 4
GOOD TRY

BABY NEW YEAR

I don't need to welcome in the new year. . . . I liked the old year fine. But Mom tells me I have to expand my horizons as I get older. She says I have to grow. Okay— let's have the sleepover at *my* house. I call Eric . . . he says no way. It was his idea, he thought of it first, and besides, he's never spent a night away from home. Bummer!

MY STUFF

MY MOM

MY HOUSE

ERIC'S HOUSE →

ME →

THE UNCHARTED FRONTIER OF SPACE

17

CHAPTER 5
REST IN PEACE

That night I have a nightmare. I'm sleeping in a lot of strange places—on the school bus, at school, on third base at the ballpark. The weirdest one is in a mattress store. Just as I fall asleep, Eric marches in blowing horns and throwing confetti, and buys the mattress I'm on.

19

I wake up. I'm home in my own bed, and that's where I'm going to stay.

UNCOMFORT ZONES

BEING WITH KIDS YOU DON'T KNOW

USING SOMEONE ELSE'S GLOVE

GETTING A NEW TEACHER

TAKING CARE OF YOUR COUSIN'S DOG

WHEN A GIRL SAYS SHE LIKES YOU

WHEN YOU SPEND THE NIGHT AT A STRANGE HOUSE

21

CHAPTER 6
SPACED OUT

Maybe I'll go for a little while before it gets dark. Mom assures me I can call her anytime, and she'll come and pick me up.

THE BEST "COME AND GET ME" EXCUSES KNOWN TO MANKIND

23

So we pack my bear, my baseball glove, my pillow, my blanket, and one video game into an overnight bag. Mom draws the line at my bed and my dresser.

An *overnight* bag . . . scary! I'll just call it a knapsack. We put it in the car and drive over to Eric's house. Actually, he lives around the corner. But still it's foreign soil. It could be Tibet. It could be outer space. Mom drops me off on the moon. I stand and watch her shuttle blast off. I feel like an astronaut, abandoned and alone.

MOM, I THINK I HAVE A FEVER.

25

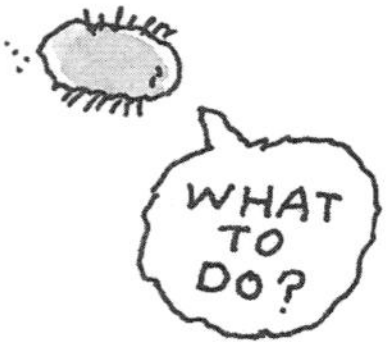

CHAPTER 7
CHECKERS MATE

Eric comes out and grabs my bag.

"Come on in, Hubie—all the guys are here."

Sure enough, there's Derek, Freddy, and Randy. They all look a little spacey, as if they just landed on another planet.

27

"Let's play a game," says Eric. He takes out the checkerboard, and we all sit around the kitchen table.

28 FISH OUT OF WATER →

I feel a little better already. Eric's mom makes hot chocolate and chocolate chip cookies. I'm feeling better all the time. At least there's a mom around in case of an emergency.

A SMALL DINOSAUR $\left(\begin{smallmatrix} EXACT \\ SIZE \end{smallmatrix}\right)$ →

CHAPTER 8
NEW FEAR'S EVE

The game is over, the hot chocolate is cold, the cookies are gone, and it's getting dark outside.

"I want to go home! It's time to call Mom."

VERY POLITE ↙

> MRS. PORTER, MAY I USE YOUR PHONE?

> ARE YOU GOING TO CALL YOUR MOTHER?

> YES, IF THAT'S ALL RIGHT.

30

"Wait," says Eric. "I have a new video game."

We go into his bedroom. It looks different. I can see the floor. His mom must have made him clean his room for New Year's.

WHOSE ROOM IS THIS?

MINE, SILLY.

CRACK!
ZAP!
POP!
ZOOM!

I'M IN THE WRONG BOOK.

ME, TOO.

31

Anyhow, his new video game is way cool.

It's called Nerds in Space. Eric explains the rules. We play it, and he wins.

It's really dark now, almost my bedtime. I want to go home. I get up to find the phone.

CHAPTER 9
GOING TO THE DOGS

"Wait," says Eric. "I have a great joke."

I can't pass up a great joke, so I sit back down. It's called a shaggy-dog story. It's about a guy who lives in Siberia. I might as well be there.

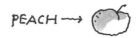

PEACH →

He grows up eating this special peach pie. He loves it, but when he's twelve his family moves to America. He learns English, does well in school, goes to college, becomes a doctor, gets married, and has beautiful kids.

WE'RE HERE, PAPA.

35

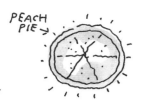
PEACH PIE →

CHAPTER 10
PIE IN THE SKY

His life is perfect except for one thing—he misses that Siberian peach pie he had as a boy.

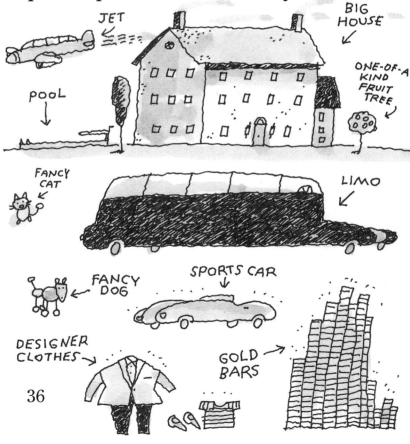

JET

BIG HOUSE

POOL

ONE-OF-A KIND FRUIT TREE

FANCY CAT

LIMO

FANCY DOG

SPORTS CAR

DESIGNER CLOTHES →

GOLD BARS →

36

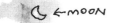

He thinks about it all the time. He can almost taste it. He moons for it, he longs for it, he yearns for it, he pines for it. One day he can't take it any longer. He leaves everything—his life, his wife, and his job. He walks out the door and heads for Siberia, which is difficult because he lives in Cincinnati.

"Eric, could you shorten this joke a little? It's getting late."

"Hubie, it's supposed to be long—it's a shaggy-dog story."

"Eric, give it a haircut."

ERIC

"Okay, okay, but it's not the same. Well anyway, he spends the rest of his life getting back to his little village in Siberia. He crawls into town and drags himself into the bakery. He looks up with tears in his eyes, and with his dying breath asks for a piece of Siberian peach pie.

DRIVE-THROUGH

BAKERY

OPEN

I MADE IT, PAPA.

SWEAT→

TEARS

DROOL →

"The baker's wife looks down and says, 'Sorry, we just sold out of peach pie.'"

"Shorter, Eric, shorter."

"This is it. This is the punch line. The guy looks up and says, 'That's okay, I'll take apple.'"

41

CHAPTER 11
A FEATHER IN HIS CAP

I look at Eric. He's laughing. I look at Derek, Freddy, and Randy. They're not laughing. I look back at Eric. It's now 10:30. That joke took two hours to tell.

"Don't you get it?" giggles Eric. "I'll take *apple*."

I want to punch Eric. I guess that's why they call it a punch line. I'm not violent, but I take my pillow out of my overnight bag and hit him with it. He grabs his pillow and hits me.

 ← LEAF FEATHER→

"I'll take apple!" he shouts. All the guys grab their pillows and soon the room is full of feathers.

GULP.

BUG →  👁 ← EYE

CHAPTER 12
THE APPLE OF MY EYE

We are all exhausted now. We lie on the floor laughing.

"I get it," I say. "'I'll take apple!'" We all laugh till tears roll down our cheeks.

 FRUITS

PINEAPPLE

ORANGE

PEAR

BANANA

CHERRY

STRAWBERRY

POTATO

APPLE

LEMON

PEACH

WATERMELON

COCONUT

GRAPEFRUIT

RASPBERRY

PLUM

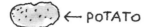 ← POTATO   COCOON →

Eric's mom comes in the room. "What's so funny, boys?"

> BOYS, DID ERIC TELL YOU THAT SILLY SHAGGY-DOG JOKE?

> HUBIE, TAKE THIS BOX.

NEW YEAR'S PARTY STUFF

We all start laughing again. She hands us party hats, horns, and bags of confetti. Then she walks out of the room, shaking her head.

49

CHAPTER 13
RESOLUTIONARY

"Well, I guess we're ready for New Year's," I say.

"Wait," says Eric, "we haven't made our New Year's Resolutions."

"Is that anything like the French Resolution?" I ask.

"A little, maybe," says Eric. "It's making promises of how you will change your life in the new year."

?

SOMETHING TO CONSIDER.

FAMOUS BROKEN RESOLUTIONS
I'LL GET A DAYTIME JOB.
COUNT DRACULA
I'LL NEVER GET A HAIRCUT.
SAMSON
YOU'LL NEVER GET ME UP IN ONE OF THOSE THINGS.
CATERPILLAR

"Eric, will you promise not to tell any more jokes?"
"No," says Eric.

"Will you promise to stop worrying about everything, Hubie?"
"No."

"Freddy, will you promise to go
on a diet?"
"No."

54

"We're not doing so well," I say.

"Maybe we can find revolutions we can keep," says Derek.

55

"How about we all promise to be best friends forever?" I say.

"Now that's a good resolution," says everyone.

"Okay," says Eric, "we're ready for the new year." But it's only 11:15.

57

CHAPTER 14
NOT ON THE BALL

So we crawl into our sleeping bags, adjust our party hats, and hold tight to our horns, waiting for the new year. But soon we are all fast asleep.

Well, to make a long story short—the ball dropped without us. We blew our horns and threw our confetti the next morning.

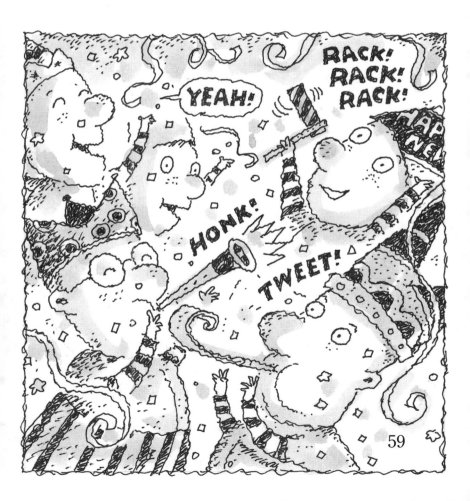

WHAT WE THINK HAPPENS AT MIDNIGHT ON NEW YEAR'S EVE

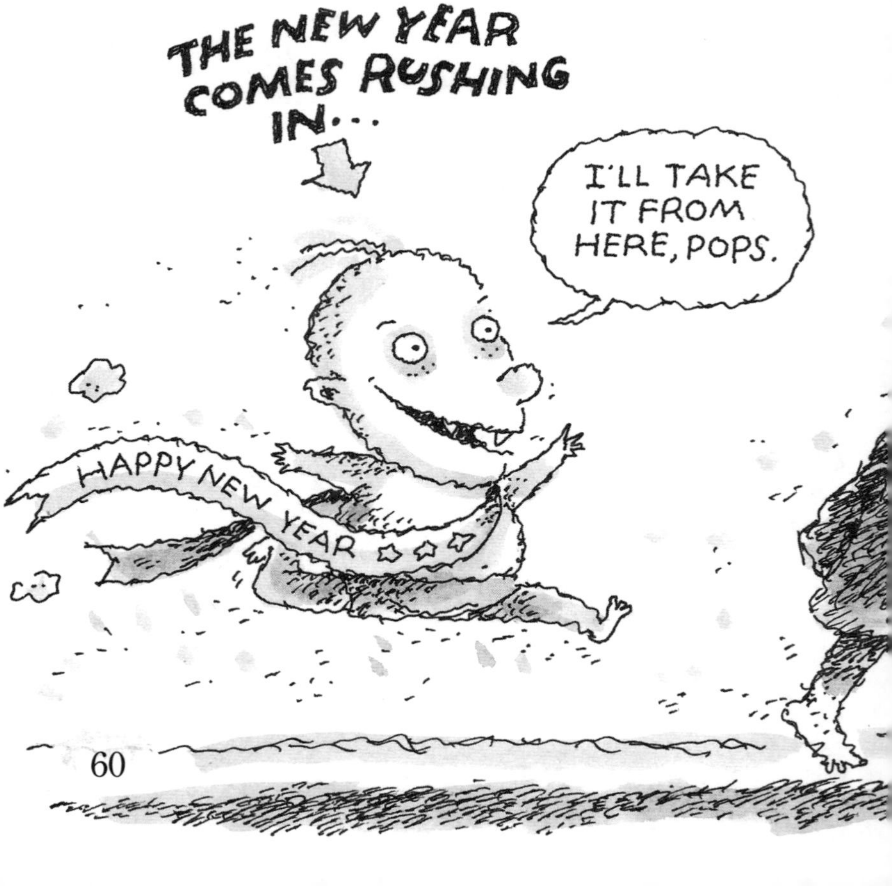

61

Eric's mom made us a big breakfast and we all resolved to stay up next year to see the ball drop.

That was fun! Next year we'll have another New Year's Eve sleepover, but I really hope it will be at *my* house.

THE VAST
UNKNOWN

MY
HOUSE